The Blessed Pomegranates

Bushel & Peck Books is a family-run publishing house based in Fresno, California, that
believes in uplifting children with the highest standards of art, music, literature, and ideas.
Find beautiful books for gifted young minds at www.bushelandpeckbooks.com.

Our family is dedicated to fighting illiteracy all over the world. For every book we sell,
we donate one to a child in need—book for book. To nominate a school or organization
to receive free books, please visit www.bushelandpeckbooks.com.

Type set in Temeraire, ChiQuel, Henman, and Basmala.

LCCN: 2023933362
ISBN: 978-1-63819-149-0

First Edition

Printed in Mexico

1 3 5 7 9 10 8 6 4 2

The Blessed Pomegranates

A RAMADAN STORY ABOUT GIVING

 A. HELWA

INTERNATIONALLY BESTSELLING AUTHOR OF *SECRETS OF DIVINE LOVE*

ILLUSTRATED BY DASRIL IQBAL AL FARUQI

SUNBEAM

Adam and Alyah were lying under a magnificent pomegranate tree. Its branches reached high above, its green leaves dancing like butterfly wings under the Ramadan sun.

Salam, it seemed to whisper. *It is the holy time of giving.*

Grandma Essi smiled. "My grandchildren, who will climb this beautiful tree and pick some fruit for me?"

"Me!" said Alyah.

"Me, too!" said Adam.

They climbed up the branches to find the pomegranates twinkling like sun-kissed rubies.

Some were crimson red. Others purple
like the sky at iftar. And some were as big
as melons! All of them went plunk and
plop into Grandma Essi's basket.

Plunk, plunk, plop!

"Subhanallah, how wonderful," said Grandma Essi. "But we have far more pomegranates than we can eat. What should we do with all these fruits?"

"Maryam loves pomegranates," said Alyah. "I can give her some!"

"So does Uncle Shakir, and Mrs. Jones, and Musa and Zuzu," said Adam.

Grandma Essi smiled again. "Ramadan is a holy time for giving. It is also when Allah revealed the verses of the Qur'an to the Prophet Muhammad, peace and blessings be upon him. The Qur'an is filled with Allah's guidance, love, and kindness. Because He shared with us, we too can share with all our neighbors, family, and friends."

Grandma Essi and Adam put
the heavy basket of pomegranates
on Alyah's cart, and together they
walked down the road.

The Ramadan sun rose high in the sky, and the wagon's wheels squeaked cheerfully as they went.

Salam, they seemed to say. *It is the holy time of giving*.

The first house was Maryam's.
"Pomegranates!" said Alyah.
"Mmmmm, delicious!" said
Maryam. "I know just the thing
to do with these."
She dropped some
pomegranates into a bucket.

Plunk, plunk, plop!

"Ramadan Karim,"
said Grandma Essi.

Next was Uncle Shakir.

"As-salamu 'alaykum, Uncle Shakir!" said Adam. "We brought you some pomegranates we picked from Grandma Essi's big tree."

"Wa-'alaykumu as-salam, Adam," said Uncle Shakir. "I know just the thing to do with these."

He dropped some pomegranates in a pail.

Plunk, plunk, plop!

"Ramadan Karim," said Grandma Essi.

Next came Mrs. Jones.

"Hello, Mrs. Jones," said Alyah. "It's the month of Ramadan for Muslims, and we celebrate by sharing our blessings with others. Here are some pomegranates for you!"

"How wonderful!" said Mrs. Jones. "I know just the thing to do with these."

Alyah dropped some pomegranates in Mrs. Jones's special shopping bag.

Plunk, plunk, plop!

"Ramadan Karim,"
said Grandma Essi.

Last was Musa and Zuzu.

"As-salamu 'alaykum and Ramadan Mubarak, Musa and Zuzu!" said Adam. "We brought you pomegranates from our grandma's tree."

"Wa-'alaykumu as-salam," said Musa.

"They are so big!" said Zuzu. "Mom will know just the thing to do with these."

They dropped some pomegranates in a large pan.

Plunk, plunk, plop!

"Ramadan Karim," said Grandma Essi.

They walked back to Grandma Essi's
house. The Ramadan sun sank low in the
sky, painting Grandma's tree red and orange
like a giant pomegranate itself. Birds rested
in its swaying branches.

Salam, they seemed to
sing. *It is the holy time
of giving*.

"All our pomegranates are gone," sighed Alyah.

"I wish we saved one for ourselves," said Adam.

"My grandchildren," said Grandma Essi, "in the spirit of Ramadan, we shared our gifts with others. Allah always rewards kindness with more abundance. Allahu Akbar. You'll see insha'Allah."

They reached Grandma Essi's
door as the Ramadan sun set
behind the mountains. The
moon rose, the azan called all to
prayer, and everyone sat down
to have iftar on this special
night. Adam and Alyah looked
at the table . . .

. . . and gasped. There were dates and walnuts, olive bread and haleem, samosas and chicken soup, but best of all,

there were pomegranates everywhere!

Some pomegranates were ripe and ready to eat, just like Maryam liked them. Some were made into pomegranate syrup, Uncle Shakir's specialty. There was pomegranate stew from Mrs. Jones, and iced, sweet pomegranate juice from Musa and Zuzu. "Subhanallah," Adam and Alyah exclaimed. "You did know what to do with our gift!"

Grandma Essi wrapped her arms around her grandchildren. "Alhamdullilah," she said. "Allah's love and mercy embraces everything He's created, including you. When you share your kindness with others, you show Allah you are thankful for all that He has given you. It is your kind hearts that have filled our table."

The Ramadan moon rose in the sky. Outside, the pomegranate tree glimmered under the stars.

Salam, it seemed to say. *It is the holy time of giving.*

And it was.

Words and Phrases

Allah: God; The Creator of everything. The One that created you with love!

Allahu Akbar: This saying translates to "Allah is the greatest." It is often used an as expression of faith or joy.

Alhamdullilah: This word translates to "All praise belongs to Allah." This word is often used to show gratitude.

As-salamu ʻalaykum: This means "Peace and blessings be upon you." This is a traditional Islamic greeting to which the receiver replies, Wa-ʻalaykumu as-salam, which means "And peace and blessings be upon you, too."

Azan: The call to prayer. During Ramadan, the azan for sunset prayer (maghrib) signals to those fasting that they can break their fast.

Bismillah: This translates to "In the name of Allah" and is often the short form of Bismillahi Ar-Rahman Ar-Rahim, which means "In the name of Allah, The Most Merciful, The Most Gracious." Muslims often begin tasks such as eating or working with bismillah.

Iftar: The meal you eat when you break your fast at sunset.

Insha'Allah: This means "If God wills." This phrase is a commonly used when setting an intention to do something.

Mashallah: This means "Allah willed it." This word is often used to show appreciation for someone or something that has happened by giving the glory to Allah first.

Prophet Muhammad (peace and blessings be upon him): The final prophet of Allah, sent to whom which the Qur'an was revealed.

Qur'an: The holy words of Allah sent to guide us to know Allah and to be kind and loving human beings.

Ramadan: The ninth month of the Islamic calendar, which is also when the Qur'an was revealed to the Prophet Muhammad, peace and blessings be upon him. Muslims celebrate this month by fasting from when the sun rises to when the sun sets.

Ramadan Karim: This means "May you have a generous Ramadan." This phrase is a common greeting during Ramadan.

Ramadan Mubarak: This means "May you have a blessed Ramadan." This phrase is one of the most common greetings during Ramadan.

Salam: It translates to "peace" but is often used as a general greeting that is similar to saying "Hello!"

Subhanallah: This means "Glory be to God." This word is often said when we are amazed by something that Allah created or has done.

Suhoor: The meal you eat before you begin your fast at dawn.